BURNING IN PARADISE

BURNING

IN

PARADISE

MICHAEL
MADSEN

INCOMMUNICADO PRESS
P.O. BOX 99090 SAN DIEGO CA 92169 USA

©1998 Incommunicado
Contents © Michael Madsen

ISBN 1-888277-06-8
First Printing

Cover photo by David Harrison
Back cover photo by Lance Staedler
Art direction and book design by Gary Hustwit

Photos on pages 12, 144, 159 by Lance Staedler
Photo on page 112 by Tony Friedkin

Mr. Madsen thanks: my wife DeAnna, Gary Hustwit, Lance Staedler, Isabelle Snyder, Amy Berg.

Printed in the USA

CONTENTS

*Dedicated to the memory
of Sam Peckinpah*

FOREWORD

Madsen.
Poet.

I like him better than Kerouac.
Raunchier, more poignant.

He's got street language.
Images I can relate to.

Blows my mind with his drifts
of gut-wrenching riffs.

This actor is a poet.
Our best.

I'm proud to know
him a little.

His words show me
a lot about me.

A laugh. A tear.
He talks of now.

Thanks Michael.
Keep enjoying the work.

I do. I love the work.

Love,

Dennis Hopper

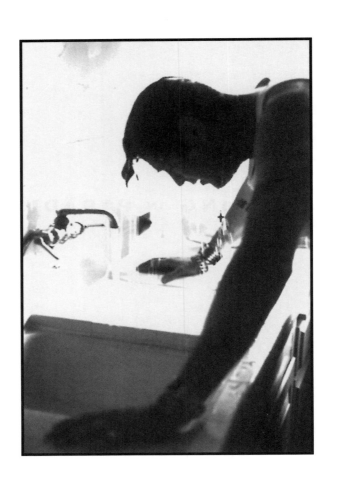

BURNING IN PARADISE

ZIPPO

I pour another shot
of vodka
and see my reflection
on the back
of a silver Zippo.

Like a mirror in
an amusement park,
a little crooked,
a little strange.

Never underestimate
the value of a Zippo.

WHITE HAIR

I figure I got
about 10 years left
to chase away
the old man.

I've seen him
late at night and
in the morning
after too much whiskey.
That's wish-key.

Maybe it's my father
I see or my dead brother.
Each man in his own way
must do this I guess.
The smart ones anyway.

I can still run faster
than a speeding bullet
and I know Superman
had a cigarette
once in a while.

GOOD-BYE

The first time I had sex
with a woman
I was 13 years old.
Her name was Jackie.
She said she was 28.
It wasn't only me
she fucked but
all my friends too.
Of course I brought
them over there but
only because they
didn't believe me.
And we all needed
to get laid you know.
Jeff, Danny, Tim, David
all got Coca-Colas
waiting for Jackie
in the white hallway.

She was married
and told us,
so we waited one day
and watched her
husband come home,
getting out of his car
and walking up the sidewalk.

All he saw was five boys
sitting on the roof
of the building watching
him waddle up.

The sad Christmas tree,
the dirty dishes in the sink,
Jackie's laundry and
broken tape deck.
The Flintstones on TV
while we sucked her tits
and she took us
one after another.

We heard she was moving
and watched from the roof
when they loaded the U-Haul,
finally driving away
she looked back up
and waved good-bye.

RAIN

Chicago, July 2, 1992,
I stuck my head out the window
into a beautiful rainstorm
and got my face and hair wet;
it was a nice welcome home.
The rain I mean.
The weathermen grumbled
like groutheaded goat snappers
so I turned the TV off.

The American flag wet
and flapping in the wind below me
reminded me of my father
who was born on July 4th
and named after the president of his day.

I saw a parking lot attendant
walking across his lot in
yellow rain slickers,
then a big fat guy in a white shirt,
black tie and black pants,
you could tell he wanted to run,
but he knew he'd look stupid
with his fat bubbling up and down
so he kept walking and
kept getting wetter.

I was wet now as were my boots
by the window, and I felt like
a seed in Death Valley waiting
for my gut to sprout.

I left the window open,
drank two vodka tonics,
lit a cigarette and
didn't move my boots.

EDGE

I went to Dupars
on Ventura Blvd for breakfast.
Sitting at the counter smoking
waiting for my french toast and bacon.
The yakkity yak yak, talk talk,
dishes clank, cups rattle
bullshit flying like the blue angels
all around me suddenly became
so loud that I knew
the crap in my life had
driven my head over the edge,
my wife, my job, the city,
the fucking french toast.
I made it back to the parking lot,
lit another smoke and drove off.

DOGS AND CATS

I woke up at 5:28 P.M. in my bed
at the Shilo Inn and realized
I had been dreaming about
my mother's dog and my sister's cat.
Griff was his name
and the cat was Sasha,
both animals were dead now
for some 10 years,
Griff even longer I think.

I was struck with such
a profound sadness at
their passing that
at that moment my stomach
began to ache and I cried.
Knowing the time that had
gone by seemed longer
than any time has ever been.

One of Griff's selling points
at the time we got him was
that he would chase
a plastic-wrapped Gaine's burger
when rolled across the floor
and open it himself being careful
not to eat the plastic, spitting out
each piece before tearing away again.

As kids we thought this was great
and having a long hallway

in our apartment, we'd roll
that burger for him over and over,
even fight about who got to do it.

At night I would see him alone
on the ledge of the window
looking down from 3 floors up,
with a look that was
somewhere far away.
I don't think he ever understood
why his owner gave him away to us.
A look that you would only
understand if you'd seen it.
And my sister's cat Sasha
jumped out that same window
one day and survived the fall.

When Griff got old we were
long bored of the burger roll
and would just drop it
on the floor and walk off.
Then we only argued about
who remembered to do it.
And I was away when he died.
I remember Sasha dead
and wrapped up in a towel
Virginia brought it over to show me
and we buried it behind
my house in Los Angeles.

I got up to write this
and don't know why
I had the dream now.

I only know I miss them,
Griff and Sasha,
I miss them more than
some people I've known.
I would like to roll that burger
for him now,
a few hundred thousand times
and hear Sasha purr
and watch her sleep
on my sister's pillow.

JACK'S

I had this job at a gas station,
it was called Smilin' Jack's.
The owner was a rubber body
lump of ignorance who thought
he was teaching me grand lessons
on manhood, things that I knew
years before I set foot in his
hole on Dempster in Evanston.
"You got a answer for everything,"
he said, well, with him there
in that place it wasn't
too hard you know.
He told me to smile more,
said it "changed my whole face,"
so I went in the shitter
and looked in the mirror,
smiling from different angles,
again and again,
trying to see what he meant.
Ding ding the hose bell rang outside,
I had a customer.

DON

My Uncle Don died a while ago.
I hadn't seen him for years.
He only had one leg.
The other one came off in
a motorcycle accident, I was told.
In fact, the day he dropped he was
supposed to pick up a new peg
or whatever the hell you call it.
His son had fought in the Vietnam War,
Bronze Star, Distinguished Flying Cross,
Medal of Honor.
Came home in one piece.
Don said he wasn't going to
a garage sale down the street.
Well, I guess he meant that.
I keep thinking about
the sad wooden leg, waiting there
wherever the hell you get them.
I was thinking of trying to get it
and making a lamp out of it
or something.
With a red, white and blue shade.
I'll miss you, Don.

SLING SHOT

There was a girl in my class named Donna,
I think it was fourth grade
and I had a thing for her
but she wouldn't talk to me.
Anyway, I had a wrist-rocket sling shot
that I was very proud of but I had to
keep it in the bushes next to a church
on the corner by my father's house.
I went to get it after school one day
and here comes Donna, walking,
walking home right down the fucking street.
I said, "Hey, Donna," but she just kept on
walking so I looked around for a rock
and loaded up the wrist rocket.
"Hey, Donna," I called again, but this time
when she didn't turn around
I let go a good shot that hit her
right in the back, dead center.
Impressed with myself, I got another rock.
This time I shot first and then said,
"Hey, Donna."
Just as she turned around
the rock hit her right in the face.
She started crying and ran out of sight.
So now I'm thinking, well,
I got her attention but I'm fucked.
So I dug a hole in the dirt under the bushes
and buried the murder weapon.

A while later I went home and then
came the grim knock on the front door,

which my father answered.
I could see from the top of the stairs
Donna with some guy
who turned out to be her father.
Her cheek was all purple,
so I thought this is good,
I didn't get her eye or anything.

Anyway, the two dads yelled
a little bit at each other
and my ass was ready for kicking,
which no time was wasted getting to.
I got slammed, punched, slapped,
saw stars and woke up in my room,
got up and walked over to the window
and looked out into the backyard.
My father was tossing some grass seed
on a place that just didn't want to get green
and my mother came out the backdoor
and stood for a long while watching
my father who didn't turn around.
Then she walked over to him
and put her arms around his waist
and they both stood there like that.
The strange thing is that it was
the one and only time I ever remember
seeing them touch.

CLINT EASTWOOD

One night in Arizona I was just out of jail
and walking across a parking lot
with a guy named Mike.
We both got released at the same time.
There were some Mexicans behind a car
and they wanted us to come over.
They had bad intentions so we kept walking.
Then Mike turned back and said,
"Fuck you, stupid spics,"
and the shit hit the fan.
I got one in a headlock and got
a few good shots to his face.
Mike ran off and the others
made themselves happy jumping on my back
and kicking the living shit out of me.
I held my own as long as I could,
even walking up the street while
they kept kicking and punching me,
yelling for me to run.
But I thought about it and didn't want
to give them the satisfaction,
so I just walked and took the hits
until they gave up.
When I got to the corner Mike was crying,
"I'm sorry, man, I pussied out,"
over and over again.
My face was puffed up
and I couldn't open one eye.
Right before we were let out of jail
I had thought Mike looked like Clint Eastwood.
All I could think of at that moment
was that he sure didn't act like him.

LOST

Highway signs and daffodils,
runaway trucks and old men
in the Catskills, the sound of rain
in the early morning
and her beautiful face.
A train in the station
waits for us to get on,
steam so thick you just can't see.
Singing songs by firelight
under the overpass
at Highway 66.

BILLY'S BIKE

It was raining outside
and I was late for work.
But I wanted to ride
Billy's motorcycle
and it was in the garage.
Pumping gas did not seem
to be so important so
I hotwired the bike and
took off onto the wet street
with no shoes on.
Too many Budweisers
maybe.

The ride was good around the block
but some lady was backing out
of her driveway on the backstretch
and I saw her at the last second
and went end over end into a gully
next to the road.
The bike was on top of my leg
and ripped off the skin of my ankle.

Someone called the ambulance
and the next thing I remember
was being in the psych ward
at the hospital
tied down to the bed.
Some guy came in looking
very self-important and asked me
if I was trying to kill myself

because of the drugs they found
in my blood tests.

I said I wanted to leave and
was now very late for work.
They put a bandage on my foot
and gave me crutches,
which I threw away
when I got home.

Billy was mad because
I wrecked his bike,
but he never rode
the damn thing anyway.

TEARS

One million tears over 35 years.

I remember Laura in her paper shoes
and paper dress, when I looked in her eyes
she was gone and I was gone.

I remember my father hitting me in the face
and falling to the floor with bright lights
flashing in my head.

I remember my mother slipping into
her bedroom with a man I didn't know.

And me fucking a woman of 28
when I was 13.

I like whores you know, there is
something pure about them.

Our shepherd jumping out
the window of the red Plymouth
and my bike getting stolen.

Sneaking out of the apartment,
down the fire escape to run around
the neighborhood with David
stealing cars and looking at the girls
in the windows of Northwestern University
watching them masturbate watching them
fuck and get fucked and dress
and comb their hair.

Flipping upside down in a '68 Roadrunner
at 2:00 A.M. going to jail in Arizona
and hearing Mark was dead

Finding out my mother was raped
and having a brother with
no marker on his grave.

Breaking into gas stations and cutting
open safes with blow torches

Breaking into houses and stealing
anything we could carry.

My father rolling up the window
of his brown Dodge and driving away
on Christmas Day.

My 6th grade teacher pointing me out
to the class and saying,
"Something is wrong here."

And a big guy I didn't know
spitting in my face and the spit
running down my cheek and chin.

Finding out my sister needed me
and not being there.

Telling my first wife I slept
with other women and seeing my father
cry at the airport while holding my son.

Breaking the door off the back
of my house and my second wife
having me arrested.

Seeing autopsy photos of John Kennedy
on *60 Minutes* and shooting a rabbit
in Lake Geneva.
Nightmares and daymares and
anytime-mares chopping off dead cats' heads
and smashing frogs with big rocks.

Having to take a shit in front
of 22 men while in jail.

And hearing Kenny Fisher hung himself.

Ben is dead Phil is dead
and Marty burned up in a fire.

Losing my job, losing my wife,
losing my money
and losing my soul.

Snorting cocaine with C. B.
and firing off a handgun through the roof
on New Year's Eve.
Standing alone on the beach
and fucking up my leg
in a motorcycle accident.

I've been shot sewn up blown up x rayed
drugged up tied up locked up fucked up
burned, stabbed, left hit, and hit back.

Alone in a room full of people.

And alone writing all this stuff.

One million tears over 35 years.

CHRISTMAS

I worked at a Christmas tree lot
sometime in the early '70s,
the exact year I don't remember,
and who really gives a shit,
anyway my boss was a real prick
who cashed in on X-mas every year
and could care less about
my skinny freezing ass. "Smile,"
he said, "You got to smile more,"
something I'd heard before
and since many times.
I guess people like me better smiling
which is why I don't very much.
"If you want to sell those trees
you got to look happy, make people like you."
All I really wanted to do was
smash him in the face but I stood
and I froze and I walked and I sold
and I loaded, while he sat in his
heated trailor like King Tut smelling
his own farts I imagined.
My mother was working two jobs.
It was Christmas Eve we didn't have a tree.
So later that night after all the station wagons
had loaded with the halfsucked lollipops
stuck on the inside of their back windows
and driven away and the lights were out
in the city, I went back to the lot,
climbed over the back fence and stole a tree.
I dragged it down the alleyway all the way
back to our place and put it on

the back porch of the first floor
of the shitty two flat
we were soon to leave from.
It was snowing outside and I looked
at the tree leaning there alone and thought
about my mother and sister I thought about
my boss the farting king prick and my father
missing another Christmas with us
and my mother not having any money
and my sister with Marilyn Monroe posters
on her wall and how happy I was
for ripping off that tree and I smiled.

CHICAGO

What kind of words do people say
when they look past the reason.
The way they walk when
the day starts out.
And night comes and the light changes,
people ask what time it is.
Looking out the window
I see a man walking a dog.
A small boy in Tokyo falls
and skins his knee.
Delta takes off for Montana
and America West goes back
to Phoenix and night comes
when the light changes
as the sun gives up again.

MORNING

The highway stretched out
ahead of me
full of cars as far
as I could see
it looked like
a long sick snake,
overfed and poisoned.

I was tired
from no sleep
and drunk
from too much drink
and all I kept thinking about
was the ham sandwich
I almost choked on,
laughing at a poem I read
a few hours before,
a strange happy laugh
that I thought was gone.

I could see the exit sign
for Burbank but
it was so far away
it was just a
fucking green dot.

NO SLEEP

When I close my eyes,
the color blue races
through my mind,
like a silky dress
on a tall woman.

Red, spilled out
of a bucket on
a paved street.

Black, like your toenail
after you drop some
heavy fucking thing on it.

Green, like a football field
with AstroTurf in a famous
stadium where I heard
that Jimmy Hoffa was
buried in the end zone.

And yellow like
the big sunflowers
used to be,
that now dry on
Patricia's window ledge
on Detroit Ave
in Los Angeles.

RIVER

There are old wooden dock posts
that stick out of the water in Youngs Bay,
covered in thick green moss.

As soon as a relationship is realized
an end is imagined,
along the way and in between
the lies people tell each other.

The Columbia flows through here,
right out to the Pactfic.
I finished the peach I was eating
and threw the pit in the water.

DIZZY

I'm sitting in Young's Bay Restaurant,
I think the waitress went to Canada.

So I'm watching and seeing a couple
stare blank faced at their waitress
then back at each other
unable to answer her question
about dessert.
I guess it was
a deep thought process.

In front of me a woman furiously
sops up blue cheese dressing
with a french fry.

The seasons will change
before my waitress comes back,
so I think about X-rays of swans
with fish hooks in their digestive tracks
and I'm dizzy from no sleep
and it's a dizzy afternoon.

SEDONA

I got a pain in my chest
walking across the parking lot,
past the Budget truck
and the Moto Guzzi.
It was a hot day in Sedona
but now the stars were out
and the night was cool.
I put a key in my door
and went into the room
and stood for a long moment
in the darkness watching
the message light flash.
I was alone in Sedona, Arizona
and went to sleep
without getting undressed.

BOB AND SAM

Bob– "That fucker is crazy."

Sam– "Who?"

Bob– "Saddam Hussein."

Sam– "Well, I don't get it."

Bob– "They're all fucken crazy."

Sam– "Who?"

Bob– "The Iraqs, every one of them."

Sam– "You can't cure it."

Bob– "It's like a yen for pussy; you can control it, or take care of it once in a while, but it always comes up again."

Sam– "Yeah, we can always go in strong but can't seem to finish the job."

Bob– "Hey, speak for yourself, asshole."

Sam– "I'm talking about the military."

Bob– "Oh."

FUCKED

I don't like this day.

I saw a spider outside my window,
crawl fast and wrap up a lady bug.
I called an old friend and told him
to fuck himself.

My wife is not my wife anymore,
but I guess she never was anyway.

I'm watching Dennis Hopper on TV
and drinking Jack Daniels.

I don't like this day.

98 IN A 55

98 in a 55 on the 26
to Portland.

We went to the Governor Hotel
and spent $400 on two hookers
that sucked us off and left

They were laughing
and we were laughing
and it was all so strange.

So we left and went
98 in a 55 on the 26
back to Astoria.

HEATHMAN HOTEL

Fox, but all I can see is the F,
and the o, the x is below the edge
of the rooftop from my vantage point
in the window of the Heathman Hotel.
I can see pigeons, one is angry
and chasing the others.

Later that night the top edges
of a high building with a big clock on it
light up and looks fancy like
Coney Island or something.

I remember some old news footage
of an elephant getting electrocuted
on Coney Island,
because he killed a man
that fed him a lit cigarette.

The fucking cocksuckers
sold tickets to see that.

ABUSE

I saw this woman in the restaurant
at the Portland Hilton,
waving her arm in the air
like she was on the Arsenio Hall show
or something.

She needed the waiter but
he wasn't looking; I was.
Her husband sat there next to that,
like a lifeless blob of
broken-balled ignorance.

She saw me looking and
embarrassed but not changed
stopped flapping the fat paw.

The waiter came by my table
and asked if anything was missing.
"A woman," I said, "but not like
that one over there, please."

He then went over to their table
and the man asked for more butter.

LATE JUNE

I'm in Portland going back to the hotel.
From the car window I see leaves
falling from a tree on the roadside
and I think of the horror
of Marilyn Monroe's dead body.
Stiff and cold.
I had a strange dream last night
about an old man under his bed,
words about him, and the dream
was so clear when I woke,
I thought I'd write it down later,
but later came and I forgot it all
and now I'm writing this
and whatever it was is gone,
like Marilyn.

FRIDAY

A cigarette butt
flipped out the door.

The windmill turning
in the breeze.

A funny little black dog
who didn't even look over
when I whistled.

Scotch whiskey afternoon
with a sunburned neck.

WOMAN

A foot came out of the plane,
what was connected to it
was even better.
The kind of woman who
looks good when she's leaving
hotel rooms and trailors,
cars and swimming pools,
a 25ft boat called the Sea Bear
and ferryboat bathrooms.

L.A.

Stepped on roses
stapled to the floor.
Dead cats, dead rats
God help the aristocrats.

Flames fly high
in the L.A. sky,
in a city where I once
heard someone say hello.

CARRIAGE INN

Stopped in for a drink.
A guy was playing the trumpet.
No one was paying attention.

Jose, the bartender, was telling
everyone how much he liked them.

When the trumpet player saw me
looking at him, he missed a note.
And if bullshit was music,
Jose and I would be a symphony.

SHOOTING

Crumpled up Camel packs
lie with dead bugs
on the table top.
The hours go by
and I listen to the soundtrack
from *Taxi Driver.*

A moth lands on my arm
and I wonder what
he thinks of the music,
or whether he thinks at all
or whether he gives a shit
or whether I do,
or why I think it's a he.
The bug seems to stare at me
and I think maybe...
then it flies off
to the fluorescent light
bored with me,
as I am of me reading this,
venal, timeless.

TROUBLEBOUND

Two flies landed
on the headrest
of the 1970 Lincoln.

It got much better
when the sun went down.
Long days and nights,
mental breakdown.
Misunderstanding and
a need for shade.
G.M. drunk in
the Apache room,
sad but true,
Donald Sutherland
at another hotel,
Lenny the motorcycle boy.
I bought drinks
for everybody.

CHRIS McDONALD

I bought a Buffalo head
at the swap meet
in Prescott,
two guys
tried to sell me
Jackie Gleason's old suit.
Chris almost got a rifle
at a truck stop
but changed his mind.
We had drinks
at the Spirit Bar
in Jerome.
And the great, sad head
got named
General Custer
on the way home.

JOEY COYLE

On the 12:30 to Pittsburgh
US Air #94 to the 'burg,
first class.

US steel, steel town USA.
3 rivers, clean now, carp.

6-foot catfish dead
on the shore
choked to death
on a duck.

Ducain Steel Works
Sci-fi buildings 4 blocks long,
rusting now in
the winter cold.
A greasy flat glove
stuck on the floor.
12,000 men making steel
24-hours-a-day
for 30 years,
and an old sign says
"hands"
only one pair
per person
be careful.

BEER, BLOOD AND ASHES

I went to see Harry Dean Stanton
play at the Sugar Shack.

He did a song from Hank Williams
and I went up on stage
and kissed him on the cheek
after the set.

I took my girl back
to the Chateau Marmont
and fixed the bed with
beer, blood and ashes.

BIRTHDAY

I turned 35 in Luxembourg,
somewhere between Paris and Germany.
There is a red bridge here where Helen said
people commit suicide all the time,
but I didn't see anyone on the rail.
I'm here shooting a film called
A House in the Hills.
I miss my son, I miss my wife,
I have nightmares when I try to sleep,
but I like the fog in the morning.

THE DEAD

I went to the United States military cemetery
in Luxembourg and touched the marbled cross
at General George Patton's grave.
5,076 American soldiers buried there.
I walked up and down the rows of markers
and saw some dry leaves blow
across the sidewalk.
I read some names and said
a prayer in the chapel.
When I left, I heard the dead screaming,
but Patton was quiet.

LUXEMBOURG

Rain drops sliding down
the windshield crying clouds,
feeling better, I took my belt off,
dropped it on the couch,
it looked like a black snake.

I can hear the traffic on the highway,
cars driving through rain sounds
the same wherever you go.

DAD

I called my father on
the 25th of September,
he said he went fishing
and caught an 18 inch northern pike
and stayed in an old hotel
built in the 1890s,
he said he remembered the day
I was born with a broken shoulder
and two black eyes.
I told him I loved him
and when I heard the dial tone
I was glad he caught that pike.

LOVE

There is nothing quite like
a woman's pussy, you know.

If you stop and think about
all the things that have been done
in the name of
or for the sake of
or in the service of
or in the taking of pussy,
you can really just go
on and on you know.

The smell of it, the look of it,
which in some cases is not so good.

The way I've seen men grovel for it
like hennie hammer flycatchers.

I myself have chased and gotten
quite a bit of it for a man of 34,
and I don't know if that's
good or bad, but mostly
I remember it as very good.

I've fucked women on rooftops,
in cornfields, in cars and on cars
and in pickup trucks
and in houses on beds
outside and in bathrooms.
Blondes, brunettes,

black ones, white ones.
At hotels and motels and once
on the railroad tracks and even
a redhead in Spain
on the island of Lanzarote.

In changing rooms at department stores
and once in a booth of a dark bar in Denver,
on couches and tables and kitchen floors.

I think about it sometimes
when I'm ready to jump from
the 8th floor window,
crying from loneliness,
and it keeps me inside.

LONELY

Airplanes and faggots
Johnny Walker and Smirnoff
cut lemons and red beer
big boats and small boats
motels and steaks.
Blue lace underwear with
shaved pussy inside, gone.
Sliding glass door
and American Spirit tobacco.
A lot of lighters, Cervantes,
bad TV and bad scripts,
bad wine and stale Camels,
whales and seals and porno tapes.
Then I go in the bathroom
and miss the pink razor.

STUD

A white horse
on the hill
shakes his head,
rusty cars
in the dusty afternoon
broken glass on a
'68 Chevy bucket seat.

The stud on the hill
backs up against the fence,
faster, stronger
and alive with disinterest.

NIGHT

How strange and still
the night can be sometimes.

Waiting for it to rain,
hearing no drops come.

Every little breeze
moving through the screen.

Wanting the sun,
seeing no light.

Dreams riding in
like Doc Holliday.

NEW YEAR'S DAY 1994

Nat Cole sings of sleep
in heavenly peace while
in Britain news comes
of aborted fetuses
being implanted
in sterile women.

I drove my corvette
to Malibu 130 mph
last night
to wish my son
happy new year.

He was sleeping
when I got there
the next day.

Today he wished me
happy birthday
on the phone.

MY SON

Robert Young sucking on his exhaust pipe
up at the enchanted cottage.
Father knows best, trying to check out.

Bud and Kitten on *Geraldo*
talking about getting
fucked-up on heroin.

My son watched George Reeves
as Superman on Nick at Night.
I picked him up and held him high,
told him to stretch his arms
out straight and flew him
all around the house.

MAN'S BEST FRIEND

I was living in Arizona for a while
in my early twenties with
a Mexican guy named Galileo,
but he had "Ernie" tattooed
on his knuckles.
I remember looking at
my Harley Davidson tattoo
in the blue light from the television
while Ernie stuck a needle in his arm
while sitting on the couch.
The next day I pissed into a
small plastic cup and sat in the car
and he took it into the methadone clinic
to pass it off as his own.

I had a dog named Shep
who followed me always and never
had to be put on a chain.

I think Ernie was mad because his dog
was a "Sooner." That means it would
sooner leave than stay.
Anyway one night we were very drunk
and I let Galileo ride my motorcycle.
When he came back he got a rope
and made a noose and put it
over Sooner's head.
I was eating Ernie-made refried beans
from a pot on the stove and watched him
tie the loose end of the rope on

the doorknob of the back door.
He pulled it tight so the dog
had to stand on his hind legs
and he started yelling in Spanish.
I picked up the pot off the stove
and whacked Ernie square in the face
with the beans flying all over us.

SUFI MAN

Sometimes when I drink
too much vodka
my whole life seems
to have been like
the dizzy dance
of the Sufi.

I heard Cat Stevens
was a Sufi.
Maybe I should listen
to more of his music
or maybe I shouldn't
drink so much vodka

I doubt if either
of those things
will happen.

BEATING

Why do some men
ask for a beating?
You can see it in their faces,
you know: they need it.

I beat a guy
with a tire iron once
who pulled a knife on me
and it felt so good
to break the bones
in his face
and see him bleed.

I probably would have
killed him if I hadn't stopped.
I guess we will both
remember each other.

CHANGE

When the sky starts to cry,
raindrops are like tears
from heaven, I think.
Everything changes.
The cars,
the lights,
the night,
the morning,
the people,
the stink,
the hate,
the pace,
the hair
and the face.
The earth taking a shower.
The weathermen grumble
and things get wet.

GEORGE

I knew this black kid in grade school,
George Mitchell. I was new in the class
as usual having moved from place to place
after my parents split up. I should have
kicked his fucking ass right away
but I already had too much other
shit to deal with. "Give me a quarter,"
he used to say in the hall after class.
George was relentless, always pushing
for a fight. I was never one to fit in anyway
so I didn't have a lot of friends black or white.
Just wanted to be left the fuck alone.

Summer went by and the new year started
and there he was in the new class
and the shit started again. I guess it was
a pattern that lived then to be pushed
to the edge before stopping it forever.

A coward by himself, he always had three
or four guys around while I was always
going about my business alone.
But I got some fireworks from a guy
named Tom and had them in my locker.
George and his friends found out and
waited for me after school. I was in trouble
for some other shit and had to stay after
so when I went to my locker everyone else
was gone, except for George and his friends.
I got my shit and tried to ignore them

standing behind me and went down the hall.
George kicked me in the back and punched
the back of my head. I kept walking.
"Give us the fireworks," one of the disciples said.
Then I got hit some more by one then another.
I got to the stairwell and thought I'd had enough.

My first hit got George in the face which
sent him flying. Then one other jumped
on my back and I threw him down the stairs.
I guess I went completely wild because
when it was over I was the only one standing
and I left the school with all my shit.
George and his friends never messed
with me again, even tried to make friends,
but I told them to fuck off.

KANSAS CITY

Waterbeds in the basement with books
about Adolf Hitler and Wyatt Earp.

Dogs that piss on the floor and children
screaming, "Thank the Lord."

Meeting your father at the batting cages
while his wife smokes in the car.

Taking Bible lessons on the farm
while Jimmy Swaggart jerks off in a motel
with a pussy in his face.

A boy leads a lamb by a rope
while too many kids swim in the public pool
and DeAnna talks on the phone
in a red wraparound.

I'm on the other end, smoking Top tobacco
and drinking Jack Daniels, hearing her voice,
with my cock getting hard.

Even a woman who paid her young sons
five dollars to get her off sits in jail.

No one can be trusted, a lover least of all.

Thank God for the brother who drove the car
and thanks to Alexander Graham Bell.

Stock car races and old ladies named Fern
dropping dead. Mom wants to know
what Buddhists are.

From Penguin Park to the go cart track,
reggae bars and joints with cocaine,
cutting off her skirts and sewing up a blue hem.
Some comets hit Jupiter
and I said goodbye to Virgil.

Writing all this, I can't help but think
that Satan never had it this good.

CAR

'62 Buick Electra
p/w, p/b, p/s, new tires,
convertible 2 dr,
rebuilt engine,
new upholstery.

That's the way the ad read.
I sold it without thinking
twice about it.
I wonder where it is now.

LANCE

When I was a young boy my mother
took us to visit her parents, my grandfather
Lance and grandmother Lavinia.
Once they had a dog named Fritz,
a brown and white boxer.
But I don't remember him being there then.
Everybody left to go somewhere
and I was alone there. In those days
I was dying of curiosity so I started looking
through the drawers for loot.
You don't ever think about being caught
when you're young.
I found a box in the nightstand
and opened it up.

Inside there were a lot of small
pocket knives and some rings and a pen
and some small stones that must have been
from a beach somewhere, smooth and small.
Just then I heard the door open
and I looked up to see Lance standing there
very quiet looking at me sitting there
on the bed with his box.
He sat down next to me and there
was a long moment. Then he said,
"You know, you shouldn't go through other
people's things." I closed the box
and put it back in the drawer.
Lance got up to get whatever he came
back for and left.

Thirty years later he died
and my mother sent me a document
of his last will and testament.
He left me that box and
everything was in it.

THIRTY-ONE

We went to the Palace one night,
upstairs the girl serving drinks
looked like Shirley MacLaine.
I told her so.

A black guy in the men's room
sold cologne and toothpaste,
his name was Jeff.
We shook hands and checked eyes.

Shirley MacLaine's real name was Amber.
I got her number before I left.

AIRPLANE

I had a slice of pepperoni pizza
at the airport in Denver.
Now I'm on 1659 to Los Angeles
thinking about an article I saw in a magazine,
"What Ever Happened to" so and so.
It said Rod McKuen was on Prozac.
Sad, stupid fucking shit man.
I saw the promise of Christmas in
the expression of a young girl,
and I fear I've lost that promise forever.
I also saw a small cardboard box
blow by the plane on the runway
when we took off from Albuquerque.
Yesterday, last night I guess,
it started to snow in Santa Fe.
We went outside and stood in it.
I saw hostility in the face of a woman
who was with another woman.
They were lovers for sure because
I've seen the look before.
Cybervision, computer upgrades,
durable luggage, features galore.
Stylish travelers, unsurpassed comfort,
form and function voice activated;
you'll never be at a loss for words
with airline magazines.

VIRTUE

There is virtue in closing the door.
Getting away from all the shit.
Why do people think they have to
talk to you on an airplane just because
they are sitting next to you?
Just fucking shut up and leave me alone.
Yes, we might crash but I don't want
to be the last person you spoke to.
There is nothing sad about being alone.
There should be a satellite screening
of *Shane* for the whole sad world.
Don't forget to turn off
the ringer of your phone.

TAXI

Rome,
it was raining
when we entered the city,
Thanksgiving Day, 1987.

After that I'd say
that there is no better way
to meet that place,
the rain in the streets
and popped up umbrellas,
the sound of a wet city.

AGE

The eyes go first,
then the hip,
not the old,
would but the writer
be the one.
The pen gets heavy
the words have
smoked heroin.
Rise and walk maybe.
Visine,
and a shot of whiskey.
Yeah, shit.
Well, if I see the light
of tomorrow,
I'll give it another shot.
Some words are
worth waiting for.

FEB. 14

New York on Valentine's Day,
I spent some time alone.
Easter Island played a part
and Frank Sinatra was there.
New York on Valentine's Day,
a place like no other.
It rained all daylight hours back.
I couldn't have asked for more.
At five past midnight,
Valentine's will have gone
but I'll still be in New York.

MADRID

She's early afternoon cool rain,
and an after-coffee cigarette.
The Prado when it's empty
and all the sad sounds.
She's traffic in a frenzy
and paper blowing into piles,
smoky quartz in fog with
sunlight here and there.
Madrid, she's out of step always.

PRADO

People don't understand me a lot,
but the more that happened
the more I understood myself.

So I guess I should thank them.
They accomplished something
in their singleminded idiocy.

Faces, faces always passing,
each different, each looking,
all lonely, never finding.
I realized today at the Prado
why art is so important.
It can be manipulated
to reflect the time it's from,
for us to see what they hoped
we would or never could.

IGUANA

I feel in my heart a strange place.
A part of me that's lost, alone, forever
unreachable by any event or person.
Why is it there? Do I need this place?
It turns up at the most unexpected times.
Like now.

The old man had his room next to mine.
He reminded me of a turtle. He tried to
drink with everyone else, but I could hear
him puking his guts out every night.
Killing himself with drink just to feel
young for a moment.

Walls are thin in Lanzarote.
I could hear him retch in his bathroom.
Poor old bastard trying to keep up
with Fabio Tesi and Fabio trying
to keep up with himself.

NUMBER 9

I thought about leaving
this page blank
but then I figured
whatever I write
won't be realized
by most folks anyway;
they see blanks where
there are shotgun shells.

LANZAROTE NIGHTS

Little lights on each balcony,
a story behind every sliding glass door.
Next door a man speaks in German
and a baby cries at a cat scratch.
L.A. doesn't exist here.
The life and times of a lost man.
Chicago, Chicago,
where are you now?

SPAIN

From Playa Blanca to Puerta de Carmen
I can see the coast of Africa.
I bought a stiletto and a cassette player.
Nice combination, I think.
Play my tapes and flick my blade.
Joe almost flipped the car on the way home.
We both laughed so hard I thought I'd cry.
Alone, alone, always alone.
The maid brought my laundry,
 it's next to the bed. I play Lou Reed
to try and sleep, wrong choice.
The sounds of the hotel are all around me.
A married woman wants to be with me.
It makes me feel sick,
I just want to be alone.

HALLOWEEN

It's gotten to the point where
we're building strange structures
with pool lounge chairs.
Hanging dummies from the hotel sign
with flaming sparklers striking
out of the head,
waking up the whole place,
700 people, with Led Zeppelin at 3:00 A.M.
It seems right.
I laid on the bed and dealt poker to myself.
The lamp fell off the table but
the maid just walked by.
I closed the sunlight out for a while
so I could look for one-eyed jacks.
That night I drank wine
out of a broken cup.

4:00 P.M.

I saw a tanker
about five miles out,
it made a zig-zag
from the open sea.
I remembered
the dead whale
I saw on the
rocky shore
yesterday.

TIM

Today I walked around Madrid
with Robert Ryan's son Tim.
We went to the Prado
and saw paintings by
Goya and Picasso.
We talked about everything.
I asked Tim if
his father had been
happy in the end.

LUCKY

Tossing dice against the wall
in my hotel room.
Seven, ten, seven,
I was lucky today.
I smoked a cigarette,
Corona was the brand name.
I walked over and stood
in the shadows.
Looking out of the window,
a sadness came over me
I just couldn't understand.

I lay back on the cool ground
to look up at the night sky
over Lanzarote.
The songs they played were
rain on me and Meet John Doe.
I swear the clouds slowed down
to hear them too.

BUS

The streets of Puerto de Carmen,
pearls, ropes of pearls, neon disco,
seemed out of place,
men playing bocci ball
and shouting in Spanish,
one wall crushed in
at the end of a street,
I saw pictures the day before.
It was where a bus lost
its brakes and crashed.
It said a man was killed
instantly.

BAR

Two of them were
from Sri Lanka,
the third was Italian,
all the way.
So oppressed they
couldn't ask for a screwdriver.
Well, I did.
And I fixed that dishwasher,
art and life identified
in one event.
I drank free the rest
of the time there.

LOBBY

Scratching camels' necks
and watching storm clouds form.
A man swings his child around
in the lobby and I think.
Lava rocks in the pool,
a cigarette in my mouth,
I decide to write it all down
and I think.

SUNSHINE

Everett brought his wife along,
or I should say Everett's wife
chose to join him to Madrid.
She must have read his script.
Also, a lot of bare tits
around the pool today.

SCHULTZ

I was having breakfast
and there was a group
of Germans at the next table
they were all talking.

One guy looked like
Sergeant Schultz
from Hogan's Heroes
and it seemed that
no one liked him
when he spoke.

I saw him
around the hotel
many times after
but he was
always alone.

BIG MAN, LITTLE MAN

We went to lunch in a place
that had tables on one side
and a bar on the other.
It was very crowded and loud.
German, Italian, Spanish voices
all talking, chicken, steak, potatoes
and beer, lots of beer.
Over at the bar two men were
pushing each other and yelling,
cursing each push in Spanish.
The big man took off his glasses
and pushed the little man
over to the door,
the little man was wearing a hat.
Then the big man shoved the little man
out on to the street
and followed after him.
I couldn't see where they went
but the other men who watched
from the window cheered and shouted.
Then the door opened
and the big man came back in,
he was wearing the hat.
We finished lunch
and smoked cigarettes and left.
Later that day I kept thinking
of the little man walking home,
drunk, without his hat.

ROOM SERVICE

She took her birthcontrol pill with
a swallow from a screwdriver.
She walked around the room naked,
picking up roomservice plates
and cigarette butts.

I was standing in the bathroom
washing off my cock and looking
at my reflection in the mirror.
I don't know who I saw,
but at least I recognized him.

Perfect tits, but she wants to enlarge them,
great ass, leave it alone please.
I'll check it out with my tongue.
Play doctor in the bathroom then
move out into the other office.
She's hanging up her coat now,
folding my t-shirt.

WINNER

Success tools,
attitude, persistence,
effort, pride, determination,
commitment, imagination, vision.
Ceiling bulb changers
folding guest beds
and vetapproved training mats,
high efficiency vacuum cleaners
and clarity enhancing telephones.
Perseverance, risk,
personalized sports bags
and a lucite swivel stand.
Live for now, baby.

NAT

I rub the back of my neck
and wish I could look
over my own shoulder,
a strange thought from
somewhere I don't understand.

I don't want to go
where you've been,
and I don't want you to go
where I've been.
I'd like to get on with it
you know.

Nat King Cole's black face
has more character than
all the fucking stupid
fortune cookie fortunes
that don't really seem
half as good
as they used to be.

DOCK

Watched a fishing yawl
unload its morning catch,
two huge tuna and about
50 or 60 bonita.
An old man on the dock
with a sharp knife cut
a filet for himself
and put it aside.
Two other men weighed
the fish on an old scale.
Their hands were the thing
that told everything.

Playa del Papagayo,
Papagayo Beach
land out before God,
land out before man.
Papagayo strand
stretched out from
land with all
the touch of madness.

YESTERDAY

One hundred years of wind,
blowing across the salt flats.
Home movies from the zoo.
Little babies in the stroller
climbing out to choke the llamas.
Ferry across the Mersey.
Blond hair hanging in my eyes.
Separation from another place,
another time.
Backwards hats and funny sunglasses.
Vaya con Dios, my baby.
I'm gonna put this over my shoulder
and make it back to my place.

DeAnna

Beautiful woman
holding sunflowers
beautiful pure simple...
legs tiger
and black lace panties
skirt opens wide
when you're getting in a car.

All he could say was
you're a beautiful woman!
Didn't he see
the sunflowers?

BUNGALOW 4

I came home to see
her dress hanging outside
with the wind blowing it
back and forth.
I hung up the hamsters
so they could blow
back and forth too.
Everything was so cleaned up,
I felt like Neil Armstrong
stepping on the moon.
Don't underestimate
that space shit.
The dogs are moving slow
because it's so hot today
and when her face
comes in the door
with my sunglasses,
she won't ever know
how or why in that moment
she made someone happy.
The helots will
never understand.

MONDRIAN

I dreamed I was in school again
and some cocksucker was telling me
I had to change my shirt.
I woke up from that and started
pacing around the room,
trying to think of airplanes
so my hard-on would go away
and I could take a piss.
Outside I could see the lights of L.A.
shining like little diamonds looking
back at me on the tenth floor.
I stood in the dark for a moment
and wondered just who in the hell
I was and who was anyone.
I thought about President Kennedy
for some reason. Then I took a piss
and got back in bed; through the window
the city lights reflected in the dormant
TV screen and I saw the world
as a projection. The last thing I thought
about before going back to sleep
was that I bet Lee Marvin
got a lot of pussy.

HER

The slap heard around the world,
painted ladies who can't get
their hands out, no camel
in the cigarette machine
and a man with a red
bald shiny head,
a yellow street lamp
and rainbows from
lemonade piss.

The 10 freeway is open
now but nobody new drives on it.
I want to bite her breasts
through my white t-shirt
so she can laugh
and tell me to stop.

MOVIE

I was standing on the set yesterday
next to the dolly, the panahead
the panavision, pointed down at the floor
looking at Marg Helgenberger lying
on her back waiting for my boxer shorts
to hit her in the face, then my socks, one,
then the other, thrown in at
the right moment for more drama.
History to be made on stage 4
at Warner Hollywood Studios.
Everybody was getting ready to roll,
grips, gaffers, electrics, DPs and focus pullers,
actors and actresses, directors and underwear
and socks. I turned for a moment
and looked off the set, just behind me,
where reality lives, and saw one of my boots
standing upright all by itself,
one single black cowboy boot
all alone just there
with no foot in it… waiting.

CHRISTIAN

After he dumped the Lego blocks
on the bed and squashed
the rubber Free Willy,
everybody finally fell asleep
watching *The Great Mouse Detective.*
I was drinking Jack Daniels
and looked at him for a long time
lying there with his arms out
to either side looking like
Jesus in rumpled pajamas.

WALK

It was raining and I
went outside walking,
across the patio down
the steps to the pool,
with its blue bottom
and white light.
I took a slice of lime
and sucked out the sour juice.
Nobody was there at the pool,
but I knew it would
be that way.

If I stood there in the half dark
for a thousand years;
if I stood there in the rain
for a thousand years
it wouldn't be long enough.
If it could stay dark
and keep raining
for a thousand years
it wouldn't be long enough.

I lit a cigarette and watched
the steam rise off the water
in the blue pool,
like it was on fire
with no flame.
I was real wet now
but didn't give a good goddamn.
The raindrops made a snap

when they hit the sleeves
of my leather jacket
and I could hear that sound
for as long as long
could ever be.

The billboard on Sunset
for the heavyweight fight is dark,
but the red neon from
the hotel sign is on it.
The fight, "one for the ages"
it says, is over and God smiled
on big George Foreman
two nights ago.
Angels were flying
around his right hand
when he knocked out
Michael Moorer.
Everybody goes inside
when it rains.
I guess that's why
I like to go out.

CATS

Moaning in agony,
wailing with horror
at the mind fucker.
I got a Cuban cigar;
it might help.
I bought some cassette tapes
in a music store in Astoria.
The place was filled
with cats, cats, cats.
Fucking blue, red and white
ribbons hanging everywhere
in the smell of them all.
Everybody's got their
own story, you know.
I got *Ray Charles' Greatest Hits*
and some Frank Sinatra.

THE CROOKED PRINCE

I'm making Free Willy II,
but the Glenness has
slipped away,
forever, I think.

The lamp over the table
made a light on the ceiling
last night that looked
like a full moon
and I met a woman
who has a son named Aaron
with cerebral palsy
and I call him
the crooked prince.
I guess we both are,
him in body,
and me in mind.
He is more alive than me
in more ways
than I care to
think about.
But always do.

WYATT EARP

The Alamo
the Thunderbird
and the El Ray Motel
in Sante Fe.
Killer landlady gets life
on News Channel 62.
Wyatt Earp is over now
and I'm home for a while.
I took my son to buy
Christmas lights
and put them
on the house.

BULLSHIT

Mankind's refusal to accept
the result of its own folly,
the super ego that thinks
it knows everything
about everything.
Based on theory, right?
The end of bullshit
would be welcome.

The empty eyes you see
every day on TV
and the quest for validation.
But it's validation of ignorance.
Loss of love,
loss of reason,
loss of *Leave it to Beaver.*
Major Nelson had a Jeannie,
but we don't.

29

I've lost faith in humanity,
lost faith in love,
lost faith in the ability
to accommodate the notion
that Frank Sinatra won't die.
There are blue boats on the wall
and Jimmy Durante sings about
making someone happy
and Joe Cocker says
bye bye blackbird.
If you turn off the lights,
your eyes get used
to the dark.

FATE

Walter Hudson, 42,
broke a thousand-pound scale.
They say he's the heaviest
person who ever lived.
He says he just wants
to see his motherss grave,
and put his footprint
in the snow.

SPIT

The rats and cockroaches
will flourish and the Wild West
rattlesnake roundup
can't get them all.
Let's not forget
the Queen of England
let Essex die.
I look out the window
of the Shilo Inn
in Warrenton,
a place where my ex-wife
spit in my face two years before,
because her Volvo
wasn't bought from
the place she wanted.
I spit back.

OUT OF JACK

I'm watching some girl
on a balance beam on TV.
A guy on the radio
is talking about the riot
in Vancouver when the Canucks
lost the Stanley cup.
I just got off the phone
with my cousin who served
in Vietnam, Bronze Star,
Distinguished Flying Cross.
O.J. Simpson is in trouble
and I miss my sons.
The water in Fisherman's Bay
is calm from my porch
and I'm out of Jack Daniels.

UNKNOWN

My sister had Siamese cats
when we were little kids
in Illinois and one day
I brought home a stray dog
and we trapped the twins
in a corner and they sprang up
and were all over me
scratching and biting and clawing.
All I could think of was,
"God, please send me
someone to love."
And this really isn't
about cats or love.

THE DOG

I took some acid one night
with my sister's first husband.
It took awhile for it to hit but,
like, the trip it takes time,
then comes on in its own way
after you give up on waiting.
Husband one was already into
his time when I started
to see the good shit.
Glowing orange paper on
the desk and walls above the door
waving like forgotten friends.
I left and went outside into
the snow and pissed under
a street lamp. The piss made
a rainbow of colors that made me
sad when they left
after the piss was gone.

My dog was in the car
and I smoked a joint before driving off.
It was really late, like 4:00 A.M.
and a lot of snow was on the streets.
Crossing over the el tracks,
the car got stuck between the rails.
No one was around so I had to try
and push the car over the rail
but the dog jumped out of the car a
nd I thought he was gonna run off
so I tied him up on the gate.

The snow kept falling
and I kept pushing the car.

Then bells started ringing
and the gates came down on the tracks.
A fucking train was coming
and when it got closer
the conductor saw us
and made the gate go up,
but the dog had slipped
all the way to the end and now
with the gate up he was hung
like a Wild West gunfighter
that finally got caught,
swinging in the dark by his neck
with the snowflakes all around.
I tried to jump up and grab
his body to pull it down.
I got his back leg and his collar broke
and we both fell in the snow.
The train guy got out
and helped push the car off.
Driving home, I thought the night
had started off well.

BLUES SALOON

A crushed matchbook
and a blank postcard from Reno,
swinging doors like an old Western,
I needed a shot.
The Baltimore Orioles
and the Kansas City Royals on TV.

Alone at the bar, the keep
poured Johnny Walker Black.
"What's the score?" I said.
"4 to 2" was his answer.

I was just a man watching
a ball game.

TRUTH

It's raining in the kitchen
and footsteps on the ceiling
are looking down.

The going gets rough.
Truth?
I've seen it
in the waves on the ocean
and at the top of the pines.
A man?
I've seen his shadow
and looking back
from the mirror.

Spoken words looking for
a hiding place in a no man's land
that swims a river of no return.

1:43 A.M.

It's 1:43 A.M.
The holidays are upon me now,
it's that most fucked-up time of the year.
Well, let's look back:
Tommy Lasorda is out of blue.
Dean Martin is dead
and they blew up the Sands last night.
Tiny Tim died, oh well.
Mother Theresa had more surgery
and they say she'll be weak now.
My kids are another year older
and closer to the truth.
Yeltsin is sick and I payed my taxes.
I made five films,
one of which will be good.
I saw New York, Miami,
Jamaica and Canada.
Rain, snow, surf and sand.
Now at 1:57 The Greg Allman Band.
Mel Torne is sick
and Mike Tyson got beat up.
Sinatra is out of the hospital,
he said Mike needed his room.
I got another Harley and a Jag.
Morrie Amsterdam is dead
and so is all television.
Not because Morrie's gone,
it was over before that.
Life goes on
in my white V-neck t-shirt
Drinking Jack and Cherry Coke.

ALTHOUGH

All the words have not yet been written,
although all the songs have been sung.

All the points have not yet been made,
although all the plots have been worked.

All the waves have not yet come in,
although the surfers have surfed everywhere.

All the cigarettes have not yet been smoked,
although many are dead already.

All the ice has not yet melted,
although the seas are full.

All the roads have been traveled,
although more are being built.

All the thoughts have ben thought,
although not everyone will listen.

All of the dogs have barked
and all of the lovers have screamed.

All of the pictures have been taken,
although all of the paintings have not yet been painted.

All of the babies have cried,
although all of the children have not yet been born.

BURT

Burt Lancaster died today
and I sat outside
with my foot on
the Everlast punching bag
that was cut down
from the tree next door.
Too much dog shit
in the grass to use it
70-some films left behind
but the cars on Sunset Blvd.
stopped at the red light anyway.

JAMES CAGNEY

James Cagney was lowered
from the stage after his number was done
and the hatch closed above him
and he was in darkness
in that wheel chair alone
and forgotten
by some stupid fucking
film school jerk off motherfucker
whose job it was
to get Mister Cagney
out of there
and he sat alone
and cried in the darkness
hearing the dancing feet
on the floor above him
and the music
that wasn't good
and the horror of being forgotten
by someone who tells the story
to his friends while they drink
pina coladas in some ignorant dump
that they laugh in.
And now it's over
and he is gone.

But that should have never happened
Something is wrong, you see,
and I crawl on the floor
in a robe from Jamaica
and laugh the crazy laugh of Cody Jarett
and try not to cry myself.

The United States is like
a big boiling pot of shit
stirred by the ghost of John Kennedy
and he is stirring it with
a big plastic sword,
like the little ones you get
with a big martini
only it's big,
big enough to stir with,
the shit floating like
our freedom
and our souls
and our future
all in that vat
while the living politicians and the media
throw more coal on the fire
to make it all COOK
for you and for me
and for all the beautiful women
who sell their precious bodies
and God forsaken selves
to the guy with the best line
or handsome face.

Let's dance and fuck
and give it all away.
All men are pigs
and all women are whores
and when the sun comes up
someone has to answer
to our children.

DENNIS HOPPER

I adjusted my tie in the mirror
and walked out to see all the cameras
waiting for the shot to start
waiting for the light to be right
waiting for me to come out
of the men's room.

I walked past the bar and saw Dennis
standing outside leaning against the wall
at the bottom of the stairs
with his arms folded
wearing sunglasses.

I kept walking because I wanted
to get to it, you know
but for that second
I thought of Dennis.

All the years
All the things
All the people
All the ideas
All the good
All the bad
All the happiness
All the movies
All the time
All the found
All the lost
All the rain

All the pleasure
All the art
All the booze
All the blow
All the love
All the hate
All the horror
All the tits
All the ass
All the money
All the pages
All the words
All the walls
All the everything
All the sunglasses
at the bottom of the stairs
right there and right then,
maybe the most beautiful sight
I had that day.

SHIT

Watch out for the shit, man.
It's all around you:
horseshit,
bullshit,
cowshit,
catshit,
dogshit,
snakeshit,
fishshit,
birdshit,
peopleshit,
ratshit,
spidershit,
sandollarshit.
It's everywhere.
Look where you walk,
scrape off your boots,
everything and everyone's
got to shit somewhere.

Friendshit,
foeshit,
Batshit,
Noah of the Arkshit.
Everybody's got to take a shit.
Even that ole Shitter – Buster Keaton,
John Kennedy and Bob Dole.

It's easier to picture
Dick Burton on the can

than Liz Taylor
even though she had to
sooner or later

Take a shit, man.
Shelly Winters,
Nixon,
Brooke Shields,
you
and Dick Cavett
all shitting.
Just think of it.

DAD

Keep it inside, or give it up?
That's the question.
Whether it is nobler in the mind
to suffer the slings and arrows
of outrageous fortune
or to take arms against them.
I wonder sometimes if
my father will ever know me.

SONS

My sons are all sleeping
Christian, Max and Hudson.
I don't know if they will ever know
how much I love them.

O.J. Simpson is home tonight
and everything is as it should be.
The news and the media aren't done yet.
They will never be done.

SKY

I saw a strange white light
moving across the sky tonight.
The star of Bethlehem?
Everybody thinks they have
a line on God.
Damn, he's not that easy, you know.
The horses keep running
at Santa Anita
and Entertainment Tonight keeps
droning on with their crap.

TIC-TOC

The clock is ticking
for the Queen of England
and it's ticking
for Gil Garcetti.

I heard about a man
who dropped dead
while brushing his teeth.

When will it come?
Where will you be?
When the clock stops.
It ticks for you,
it ticks for me.
It ticks for Larry King.

The Discovery Channel
has a program about
the end of the sun.

THE SHIT

I was thinking about all of the crap
I learned in High School,
and I thought of fresh steaming shit
coming out of a horse's ass
on the street in New York City
squeezed out, falling, smoking,
turning, then splatting on the ashpalt
to rot in the sun.
They lied about the Indians
and everything else too.

RUN

Everybody is running.
Just like Yohan,
Herman Munster's twin.
Run, run, run.
Green face and big feet.
I saw a documentary
on O.J. Simpson.
Run, run, run.
No rain for a long while now.
Torches held by protaganists.
Run, run, run.
Lilly and Grampa,
Spot and Little Eddie with Wolfy.
Say what you will,
it's all entertainment.

TEN

I wrote ten poems tonight
and now I am haunted
with the idea of sleep.
Sleep, sleep, wonderful sleep.
Jack Daniels screaming.
Merlin the green parrott sleeping.
Old No.7 brand alcohol
43% by volume
86 proof
distilled and bottled
by Jack Daniel Distillery
Len Motlow proprietor
Lynchburg, Tenn.

NIRVANA

Nambia, I heard,
has people that have never
seen the white man.

The phrase book has yet
to be written, I guess.
They really don't need it
as their bellies swell in the dust.

We really should leave them alone,
they'd save a lot of money
on hair care products.

VEGAS

I took the elevator up to D.
Chris Penn's box
of Kodiak Tobacco
was in the breast pocket
of my jacket.
I got upstairs
into the room
and dropped a stack
of chips from
the Desert Inn
on the table.

LIFE

Showbiz magazine on
the coffee table
with a showgirl on the cover.
Bad music on the radio
and all the sad lights
blinking off and on outside.
I'm here shooting a movie
called "The Winner."
There are too many people
in the lobby
and too much noise
in the world.

MIRAGE

I can see the big
bright white letters
of the Mirage
outside of my window.
The room reminds
me of Elvis.
And I feel like Elvis
when I walk around.
The white tigers are asleep
on the lobby level
and the slot machines are
ringing,
ringing,
ringing.

PHAROAHS

In all the madness
and all the darkness,
when Satan shows his face
and he knows you're looking,
Cheyenne Brando
swings by her neck
and the horror
is all too real.

I put out my Chesterfield
in an ashtray that has
flowers printed on it
The last of the great tombs
that line the road
all the way to Athens
rot away in the sun.

BLUE

My dog makes me feel
like a Viking sometimes.
I'm a Dane, you know,
so it isn't bullshit.

Dogs have a vibe about them
Blue has it in spades.
Laying next to me at night
he's ready to bite
and kill for my sake.

He's a big, lonely old soul
black and proud.
He took off and ran
down the beach
while I was writing this,
after some dark, unseen
demon from hell.

COLES

I walked into the men's room at Coles
whistling *White Christmas.*
I was thinking of Otis Redding.
Not a lot of people
know he sang it,
but I heard the CD
and it made me whistle.
Coles, the oldest restaurant
in Los Angeles, inventor of
the French Dip in 1908.
It's old you know,
really fucken old.
But it has more class
than all the new places.
There is a big board
on the wall behind the bar
with names of professional drinkers.
My name was not there
but I think it should be.
Anyway, I'm in the men's room,
whistling,
and a cop came in,
walked by and went into
a stall to take a shit.
First, I thought he was
just going to piss
and adjust his gun.
But I soon realized
he was gonna shit
while I whistled
White Christmas.

MICHAEL MADSEN was born in Chicago, Illinois and currently lives in Los Angeles, California.

INCOMMUNICADO PRESS

BOOKS

Steve Abee KING PLANET 146 pages, $12.

Dave Alvin ANY ROUGH TIMES ARE NOW BEHIND YOU 164 pages, $12.

Dave Alvin THE CRAZY ONES 156 pages, $12.

Elisabeth A. Belile POLISHING THE BAYONET 150 pages, $12.

Iris Berry TWO BLOCKS EAST OF VINE 108 pages, $11.

Beth Borrus FAST DIVORCE BANKRUPTCY 142 pages, $12.

Pleasant Gehman PRINCESS OF HOLLYWOOD 152 pages, $12.

Pleasant Gehman SEÑORITA SIN 110 pages, $11.

Barry Graham BEFORE 200 pages, $13.

R. Cole Heinowitz DAILY CHIMERA 124 pages, $12.

Hell On Wheels Edited by **Greg Jacobs**, 148 pages, $15.

Jimmy Jazz THE SUB 108 pages, $11.

Michael Madsen BURNING IN PARADISE 160 pages, $14.

Peter Plate ONE FOOT OFF THE GUTTER 200 pages, $13.

Peter Plate SNITCH FACTORY 182 pages, $13.

Scream When You Burn Edited by **Rob Cohen**, 250 pages, $14.

Unnatural Disasters Edited by **Nicole Panter**, 256 pages, $15.

We Rock, So You Don't Have To Ed. by **Scott Becker**, 256 pages, $15.

COMPACT DISCS

Incommunicado also distributes select spoken word CDs from New Alliance Records and Ruby Throat Productions. See our website for audio clips and the full list.

Exploded Views A San Diego Spoken Word Compilation, $14.

Gynomite! Fearless Feminist Porn, $14.

Available at bookstores nationally or order direct: Incommunicado P.O. Box 99090 San Diego CA 92169 USA. Inside the U.S., include $3 shipping for 1 or 2 items, add $1 for each additional item. Outside the U.S., $7 shipping for 1 or 2 items, add $2 for each additional. For credit card orders call 619-234-9400. E-mail: severelit@aol.com. For online ordering, book excerpts and audio/video clips, go to the website: http://www.onecity.com/incom/
Distributed to the trade by Consortium Book Sales and Distribution.
Please help us destroy American Publishing. Thank you.